This book belongs to:

JOSHUA McAULEY
....

HAPPY EASTER 2006
....

love Auntie Mary & Uncle Gilmore
....

Retold by Gaby Goldsack
Illustrated by Kim Blundell (John Martin & Artists)
Designed by Jester Designs

Language consultant: Betty Root

ISBN 1-84461-213-9

Marks and Spencer p.l.c.
PO Box 3339, Chester CH99 9QS
www.marksandspencer.com

Copyright © Exclusive Editions 2002

Printed in China

MARKS &
SPENCER

The Three Billy Goats Gruff

Helping Your Child to Read

Learning to read is an exciting challenge for most children. From a very early age, sharing story books with children, talking about the pictures and guessing what might happen next are all very important parts of the reading experience.

Sharing reading

Set aside a regular quiet time to share reading with younger children, or to be on hand to encourage older children as they develop into independent readers.

First Readers are intended to encourage and support the early stages of learning to read. They present well-loved tales that children will happily listen to again and again. Familiarity helps children to identify some of the words and phrases.

When you feel your child is ready to move on a little, encourage them to join in so that you read the story aloud together. Always pause to talk about the pictures. The easy-to-read speech bubbles in **First Readers** provide an excellent 'joining-in' activity. The bright, clear illustrations and matching text will help children to understand the story.

Building confidence

In time, children will want to read *to* you. When this happens, be patient and give continual praise. They may not read all the words correctly, but children's substitutions are often very good guesses.

The repetition in each book is particularly helpful for building confidence. If your child cannot read a particular word, go back to the beginning of the sentence and read it together so the meaning is not lost. Most importantly, do not continue if your child is tired or simply in need of a change.

Reading alone

The next step is for your child to read alone. Try to be on hand to give help and support. Remember to give lots of encouragement and praise.

Together with other simple stories, **First Readers** will ensure that children will find reading an enjoyable and rewarding experience.

Once upon a time there were three Billy Goats Gruff.

There was a big Billy Goat Gruff.

There was a middle-sized Billy Goat Gruff.

And there was a little Billy Goat Gruff.

The three goats all loved to eat grass.

They ate grass all day long on the hill.
But they never crossed the bridge to eat
the grass on the other side.

They never crossed the bridge because the Troll lived under the bridge.

The Troll was very bad. He ate anyone who dared to cross his bridge.

One day the little Billy Goat Gruff looked at the green, green grass on the other side of the bridge.

"I'm not scared of a silly old Troll," he said. "I'm going to cross the bridge."

"Me too," said the middle-sized Billy Goat Gruff.

"And me," said the big Billy Goat Gruff.

"You go first. It was your idea," said the big Billy Goat Gruff to the little Billy Goat Gruff.

Trip, trap, trip, trip, trap!

So the little Billy Goat Gruff set off
across the bridge.

Trip, trap, trip, trip, trap went his
hooves.

"Who is that trip-trapping over my bridge?" roared the Troll.

Who goes there?

"It's only me!" said the little Billy Goat
Gruff. "I'm going to eat the green, green
grass on the other side of the bridge."

"Oh no, you're not!" roared the Troll.
"I'm going to eat you up!"

"But I am just little," said the little Billy Goat Gruff. "Wait until my middle-sized brother comes across. He is far bigger than me."

"Very well!" said the Troll.

Very well!

So the little Billy Goat Gruff crossed the bridge. Soon he was eating the green, green grass.

Next, the middle-sized Billy Goat Gruff crossed the bridge.

"Who is that trip-trapping over my bridge?" roared the Troll.

"It's only me!" said the middle-sized Billy Goat Gruff. "I am going to eat the green, green grass on the other side of the bridge."

"Oh no, you're not!" roared the Troll. "I'm going to eat you up!"

I'm going to eat you up!

"But I am just middle-sized," said the middle-sized Billy Goat Gruff. "Wait until my big brother comes across. He is far bigger than me."

"Very well!" said the Troll.

And don't come back!

So the middle-sized Billy Goat Gruff
crossed the bridge. Soon he was eating
the green, green grass.

Next the big Billy Goat Gruff crossed
the bridge.

Quake! Shake!
Rumble!

"Who is that trip-trapping over my
bridge?" roared the Troll.

"It's only me!" said the big Billy Goat Gruff. "I'm going to eat the green, green grass on the other side of the bridge."

"Oh no, you're not!" roared the Troll. "I'm going to eat you up!"

I'm going to eat you up!

The Troll jumped onto the bridge.

The big Billy Goat Gruff lowered his horns and charged.

Crash! The big Billy Goat Gruff banged into the Troll. The Troll flew into the air. Splash! He fell into the water.

Crash!

Splash!

The big Billy Goat Gruff skipped over the bridge. Soon he was eating the green, green grass.

And the ugly Troll was never seen again.

Hooray!

Read and Say

How many of these words can you say?
The pictures will help you. Look back in
your book and see if you can find the
words in the story.

big goat

bridge

grass

hill

hooves

horns

little goat

middle-sized goat

Troll

water